Boo Loves Books

For every reader and listener
~ K B

In memory of Noah, a Very Good Boy
~ T G

Boo Loves Books

Kaye Baillie

Tracie Grimwood

NEW FRONTIER PUBLISHING

Everyone in Miss Spinelli's class liked reading.

Everyone except Phoebe.

'Phoebe, the book basket is that-a-way,' said Miss Spinelli.
'I know,' Phoebe said. 'But I like to go the long-a-way.'

Phoebe worried when she didn't know the sound of a letter.
And letters that were joined together made her freeze.

When Phoebe knew a word she stayed
quiet, in case she got it wrong.

A little later, Miss Spinelli made an announcement:
'No reading at school tomorrow.'
Phoebe whooped inside.

'Instead, we'll be reading somewhere special.
Be at school early. We're taking the bus.'

Phoebe's tummy went

flip,

flop,

flip.

The feeling
lasted all day,

then
followed
her home.

'I'll be sick tomorrow,' said Phoebe.
'Are you sick now?' asked her mum.
'A little. But I'll be much worse
in the morning.'

'Tomorrow will be a good day, Phoebe. You'll see.'

The next day, Phoebe climbed onto the bus.
She sat with her friend Harriet and stared out
the window as the bus rumbled along.

Then Harriet jumped up.

'The animal shelter!' said Harriet.

Phoebe frowned. 'This isn't
a place to read books.'

'Every place is a place to read
books,' said Miss Spinelli.

'Everyone follow the keeper,' said Miss Spinelli. Phoebe squeezed Harriet's hand as they shuffled past rows of yipping, yapping dogs.

Then they stopped.
Miss Spinelli explained how
each child would read …

... to a dog.

Phoebe was already worried about reading
and she didn't know much about dogs.

What a terrible day!

'This is your dog, Phoebe.
His name is Big Boo.'

Clutching a picture book, Phoebe followed
Miss Spinelli inside.

Phoebe stared at Big Boo.
Big Boo stared at Phoebe.
When he moved …

… Phoebe froze.

'I want to go home,' she whispered.
'I'm staying right here,' said Miss Spinelli.

'This dog is a little bit scared. But he would never hurt you.'
Scared, thought Phoebe. *Of me?*
'Talk about the pictures,' said Miss Spinelli.
'Your voice is all he needs.'

Phoebe got comfortable then
slowly opened the book.
'There are twinkling stars,
and a big red pirate ship
ready to sail the seas.'

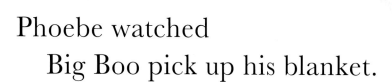

Phoebe watched
    Big Boo pick up his blanket.

'Pirate monkeys!'
Phoebe gulped as Big Boo stepped closer.
'They're fighting over treasure.'

She could see Big Boo's skin where hair had once grown.
A rubbery mouth with a droop. And eyes not scary, but soft.

'Maybe you escaped from a pirate monkey ship?
Is that what happened to you, Big Boo?'

Phoebe kept reading.
When she got stuck,
Big Boo didn't
mind one bit.

But before Phoebe finished the book, Big Boo picked up his blanket and plodded to the back of his room. 'Why did he do that?' Phoebe asked Miss Spinelli.

'He's used to people coming and going,' said Miss Spinelli. Phoebe looked at Big Boo. She realised they were both scared of things.
'Miss Spinelli, do you have a book about dogs?'

Phoebe opened the book. 'I'm staying right here, Big Boo. You'll see.'

Phoebe read in her best voice and didn't care if she got words wrong. She just wanted Big Boo to come back.

And he did.

One day at school, not long after, Phoebe announced,
'This is my new dog, Big Boo. He's the best listener in
the world. He loves books about dogs. And so do I.'